HUDDLE UP! Cuddle up!

by Bethany Hegedus   illustrated by Mike Deas

VIKING

VIKING

An imprint of Penguin Random House LLC, New York

First published in the United States of America by Viking,

an imprint of Penguin Random House LLC, 2020

Visit us online at penguinrandomhouse.com

LIBRARY OF CONGRESS CATALOGING-IN-PUBLICATION DATA IS AVAILABLE.

ISBN 9780593115626

Manufactured in China

Book design by Lucia Baez

This art was created with brush pen and watercolor.

1 2 3 4 5 6 7 8 9 10

For Dad, a Chicagoan through and through, who gives the best "Bear" hugs. And for Taru, whose dad and I love our nightly Story-Time-Outs.
—BH

For Annie and Faye.
—MD

The coaches gather their gear . . .

and the pregame warm-up begins.

Scrub.   Scrub.   Dunk.

Scrub.   Scrub.   Dunk.

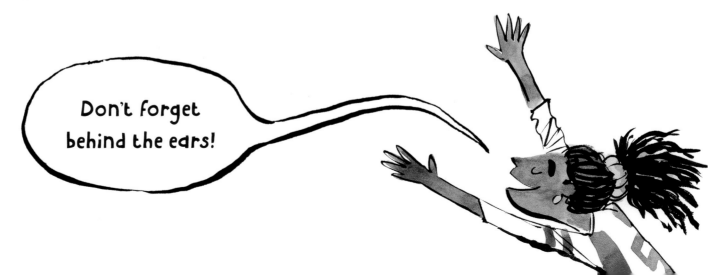

Don't forget behind the ears!

After toweling off, the players suit up.

Arm. Arm. Neck. Neck.

CHECK.

The bedtime countdown clock continues as . . .

. . . he moves to the left.
She moves to the right.
Brush. Brush. Spit.
Brush. Brush. Spit.

Keep it moving!

Coach calls the first play.

Ready . . .

Set . . .

Hike.

Nine minutes down.
Six minutes to go.
Coach calls the next play.

Razzle dazzle.

And the running back is . . .

With four minutes left, will the Dream Team make it in time?

Your guess is as good as mine.

And the countdown clock begins again . . .

And it's a . . .

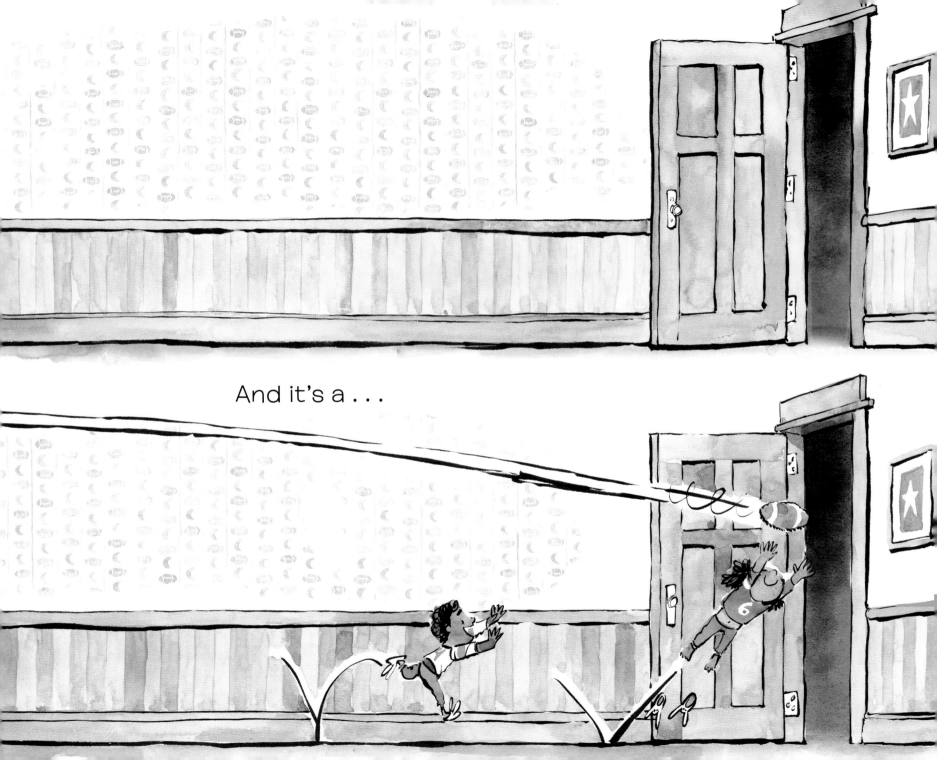

TOUCHDOWN!

And the fans go wild!

And there you have it, folks.